Jumping Jack

by Geoffrey Alan
Illustrated by Angela Mills

Brimax · Newmarket · England

"I feel full of bounce today!"
says Jack-in-the-box as he
springs out from the toybox
and bounces around the room.
"Please be careful!" says
Polly the Ragdoll.
"Slow down, Jack!" call Oscar
the Octopus and Tumble the
Teddy Bear.

The toys belong to a little girl called Katy. She has gone away with her parents. Boing! Boing! Boing! Jack keeps on bouncing. Polly has found one of Katy's ribbons and is skipping with it. But Jack bounces too close to her and poor Polly is all tangled up.

"Come back and help me," Polly calls to Jack.

"All right!" he says. But Jack does not see Tumble trying to ride Katy's scooter.

"Look out!" shouts Tumble.

"Oh no!" says Jack. He bounces extra hard and springs right over the scooter. But Tumble wobbles and then falls off.

"Oops!" he says, landing on a bean-bag.

The bean-bag bursts and all the little beans spill out.

"Oh no!" says Polly. "We will have to put them all back and sew it up again. You are a pest, Jack!"

"No I am not," says Jack. "I am only bouncing around!" This time he lands on the end of Katy's see-saw. On the other end is a big cushion. It flies through the air.

"Catch that cushion, someone," Jack laughs. But it lands on the book shelf and the books begin to slide off.

"Oh no!" yells Tumble, diving under a desk.

Polly puts up an umbrella. But as the books fall, Oscar catches them all at once.

"There is not enough room in here for you to be such a pest," he tells Jack.

"You are right!" says Jack. He bounces over to the door, springs up and opens it and bounces outside.

"We had better follow him to make sure that he does not cause any trouble!" says Oscar.

Boing! Splash! Boing! Splash! It has been raining and Jack bounces in and out of the puddles along the path.

"This is fun," laughs Jack.
"Wait!" Polly calls after him.
She is still carrying her
umbrella.
"Where are you going, Jack?"
calls Oscar.
Jack does not hear his friends
calling him. He keeps on
bouncing along the path
beside the field.

Boing! Boing! Jack bounces faster and faster.

A rabbit hops across the path in front of him.

"Look at that!" says Jack.

"He can jump almost as high as I can!"

Jack is not watching where he is going, for he turns around and bumps into the strangest man he has ever seen.

Jack springs back in surprise and lands in the middle of the ditch. SPLAT! It is full of sticky mud. Jack tries to bounce out, but he is stuck.

"Please help me out of here!" he cries to his three friends.

"How did you get in there?" asks Oscar.

"He made me jump!" says Jack. "Look!"

"He is only a scarecrow!" chuckles Oscar.
"You should not have bounced off like that," says Tumble.
"Well I cannot bounce anywhere now," says Jack sadly.
Tumble nearly falls in the ditch. "The sides are very slippery," he says.
"Then how can we rescue Jack?" asks Polly. Oscar sees her umbrella and has an idea.

Oscar wraps six of his long legs around a nearby tree. Then he stretches out the other two.

"I'll hold onto you, Polly," he says. "And you can hold on to Tumble."

"What shall I do?" asks Tumble puzzled.

"You can hold onto Polly's umbrella and give the other end to Jack," says Oscar.

Tumble is not sure that the plan will work. But they stretch out in a line, Polly holds onto Tumble with both hands.

"Grab the handle, Jack!" says Tumble. "Now all together . . . Pull!"

They all pull very hard.

At last, Jack is free.

"Thank you!" he says. "I might have been stuck forever!"

"You will need to get scrubbed in the doll's-house bathroom," says Polly. "You are very muddy!"

"I am very sorry, too," says Jack. "I promise never to be a pest again."

Say these words again

bounce	springs
tangled	extra
wobbles	sew
enough	beside
faster	across
tries	slippery